THE

FIRST

HOWL

*Dedicated to anyone big or small
that still feels like running, jumping,
getting drenched in rain, screaming
and howling!*

CONTENTS

Prologue

*Everything we know about wolves... **IS WRONG.***

Have you ever wondered why wolves howl at the Moon? What draws them to raise their heads to the night sky, and sing to it?

Maybe... it's because they come from there...

And they are expecting an answer.

Millennia ago, in a time lost in history, wolves roamed the Moon. They were called the Astorai, which in our language means "Moon Wolf", and their packs were the true sons and daughters of the Moon. Their colours ranged from the crispest white to the darkest black and every shade in between, but they all had something in common: silver flecks as bright and shiny as the Moon itself ran through their fur (and that's why we can't see them from our planet – they're camouflaged!).

But these wolves were not like the ones we know; they were civilised, and they built great cities using the very rock from the Moon. Theirs were the cosiest little houses, and no Astorai was ever cold during winter.

In time, some of these Astorai – the explorers, astronomers and adventurers – grew curious about the big blue orb they saw every night when looking at the sky. This orb was our planet, Earth, but for them, it was **The Big Blue Marble**.

And there, on The Big Blue Marble, they found things they were not ready to see. Things stirring in the shadows… Things with paws, and fur… things like them. Things like… **wolves**.

Get ready to be launched into the story of Talah; a brave, young Astorai that would change the way we see wolves, forever.

A Light in the Sky

A long, long time ago, on the Moon that you and I see at night when we look at the sky, there lived a young Astorai wolf called Talah. His fur was shiny grey with flecks of silver, like the surface of the Moon itself, and he had just turned twelve (merely the blink of an eye in the life of an Astorai, since they live very long lives).

Talah was just one of the many wolves that roamed the Moon, and there he lived with his mum, Lua, in a magnificent little lighthouse on top of its highest peak (and from there, they undeniably had the best views of The Big Blue Marble!).

But why did they live at the very highest point of the Moon? Well, they had a good reason: Lua was an astronomer! She spent her days looking through a big, **HUGE** telescope that she and her husband, Hati, had built at the top of the lighthouse. From there, she investigated the vast wilderness of space, with all its stars and planets...

But something fascinated her over anything else... she couldn't help it; she had a very special interest in one of those planets in particular – The Big Blue Marble! And while she was at work, Talah loved to play in a big crater outside their lighthouse, running and exploring all day long.

"You got that exploring spirit from your dad!" Lua would often say to Talah, fondly; but this was a bittersweet statement...

Talah had never got to know his dad, Hati, as he'd passed away shortly after he was born. But Lua was a great storyteller, so she kept her late husband's memory alive by telling Talah all about the adventures they'd had, and the discoveries they'd made together – as Hati was an astronomer as well!

There was nothing Talah liked better than jumping on that crater – as **HIGH** as he could!

You see, due to gravity, everyone is much lighter on the Moon, so Talah could almost **FLY** when he jumped. Lua had told him so many stories about The Big Blue Marble; so many exciting things about the blue planet, that he became obsessed with the idea of jumping so high that he could reach it and touch it with his snout!!! But Talah was about to learn that you should be careful what you wish for...

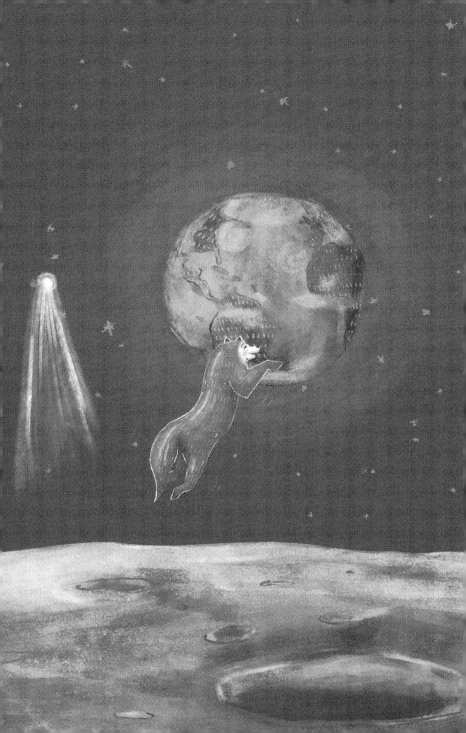

One morning, Talah was jumping in the crater, as usual, when a weird noise came from the sky. It was a **loud**, **rumbling** noise; like the sound of a freight train.

"What... what's that?" Talah wondered, as he froze on the spot and tuned his ears as finely as he could to try and identify the noise.

Just as Talah was surveying the ocean of stars and planets in the sky, a big old wolf walked by. It was Mr Thomson, one of Talah's neighbours, and quite a **grumpy** one, as far as he knew. He always wore a grey, pinstriped hat on his head... but never a smile on his face.

"Wasting your time looking at the sky again, eh, Talah?" grumbled Mr Thomson, as he walked past.

"Don't rise to it, don't rise to it..." Talah muttered to himself. He knew it was better not to respond to the old wolf. Mr Thomson loved to talk and judge much more than to listen and understand.

"I hope you soon realise that you should be doing something else with your life, sonny boy." Mr Thomson shouted from afar. He hadn't even stopped walking while lecturing Talah, and he disappeared into the distance leaving his words lingering in the air.

Talah had managed not to fall into Mr Thomson's spiral of misery, but he was feeling quite down now.

"What if Mr Thomson's right?" Talah thought. "Maybe I should stop thinking about The Big Blue Marble so much..."

But then, there it was again. That loud, rumbling noise; like the sound of a freight train... Talah's head immediately thrust back up to the sky.

Out of nowhere, a shining light appeared, glowing like a massive **FIREBALL**. Talah could swear it looked just like the stars that filled the sky, but this one was moving, and pretty quickly!

It flew like a lighting bolt towards The Big Blue Marble, blazing a trail of glowing dust in its wake. And just as it was about to reach the blue planet at an unbelievable speed, POOFFFF! It disappeared...

Talah couldn't believe his eyes. What was this weird, darting, star-like thing in the sky?

"I have to go tell mum about this!" Talah thought. "She would surely know what this thing was!"

And as fast as the ball of light he had just witnessed, the young Astorai raced back home to see his mum.

Close your Eyes; Make a Wish

Talah bolted into his mum's observatory. As usual, Lua was glued to her big telescope.

"Mum! Mum!" Talah barked, almost out of breath. "I was jumping in the crater when--when... something incredible happened!"

Lua slowly turned from her telescope; and her long white coat sparkled in the light coming from the observatory window. Looking at her exhausted son, she smiled.

"Well, judging by how far your tongue's hanging out your mouth... Did you finally jump so high that you touched The Big Blue Marble with your snout, Talah?" she giggled. "Sometimes I wonder if you aren't actually a frog in wolf's clothing!"

Talah couldn't contain himself, so he continued:

"But mum! I just saw a star move! It bolted like lighting and then it disappeared! I need to know what it was!"

Lua's expression immediately changed from amused to intrigued, and after taking a pause for thought, she said:

"Well Talah, aren't you a lucky little wolfy! It sounds as if you've seen a shooting star!"

Talah tilted his head, confused.

"These stars… they don't show up for just anyone. They say shooting stars only appear to those with big dreams… to help them become who they're meant to be." she finished.

"Really? Wow! And how many shooting stars have you seen, mum?" said Talah while scratching his head with his paw.

Lua let a small, almost inaudible laugh come out of her mouth.

"I'm afraid these are just stories, Talah… " Lua replied. "Are you sure you saw one? Maybe all that jumping got you dizzy, and then everything around you looked like it was moving!"

"No mum! I promise! I saw it so clearly! It was right there in the sky!" exclaimed Talah, as soon as his mum finished her sentence.

Lua looked Talah in the eye. The young wolf could almost see how the cogs were turning inside her head, and then she said:

"You know, Talah... even though, like me, your dad never saw a shooting star, he believed in them with all his heart... so I believe you, Son. I think it's time I tell you about a big secret I've been keeping for years. Something that could change the world as we know it, forever..."

Talah had never been as attentive of his mum's words as he was now.

"I think... I think there are wolves like us down there, Talah.... There are wolves on The Big Blue Marble." continued Lua. "Your father and I researched this for years... Come take a look, the telescope's pointing to where we thought they might be."

Talah wouldn't admit it, but as he slowly walked towards the telescope, he got a bit scared. Looking through the lens, the planet that they knew as The Big Blue Marble lay before him.

He saw a massive forest, with a big rocky peak taller than any of the trees in the centre of it.

"There, Talah, in those woods your dad and I discovered things moving through the trees. I can't be 100% certain they are wolves, but my heart tells me they are." Lua said, gazing out of the observatory window.

This forest fascinated Talah. It was covered in mist, and for a second, he could swear that he too saw shadows moving through the trees... **Wolf shadows**.

Talah stepped back from the telescope, his jaw almost hitting the floor in awe.

"Everyone should know about this! You should show this to the other wolves!" Talah exclaimed.

"That won't work, Talah. Believe me." replied Lua. "Your dad and I already tried to convince the others once, but they wouldn't listen. They thought of us as lunatics, they laughed at us...

No, Talah, if we want them to believe us, I would have to go to The Big Blue Marble and back to prove it... but I just can't see a way of doing that..." she trailed off, her face showing both frustration and sadness.

Leaning closer to his mum, Talah rubbed his head against hers, as the Astorai do when they want to hug each other. Lua exhaled deeply, and continued:

"I've never seen a shooting star, Talah... But if I did, I'd wish it could help me prove that we're not alone – show the rest of the wolves that we are not alone... I'd wish I could prove that all your dad's efforts weren't in vain."

The Adventure Begins

Many days had passed since Talah had discovered the secret about The Big Blue Marble; and he'd spent them in his favourite crater, as usual. But now he wasn't running, he wasn't exploring... he wasn't even jumping. Talah just sat in his favourite spot staring at the blue planet, mesmerised, asking himself the same questions over and over.

"Why are there wolves on The Big Blue Marble?"... *"How did they get there?"...*

"What was that shooting star trying to tell me?"...

"...What are we having for dinner tonight?"

The Big Blue Marble looked especially big tonight, and Talah knew why. Ever since he was just a cub, Lua had taken him on camping trips to beautiful craters, hills and endless plains. And on certain special nights, while they were both looking at the sky, Lua would always say:

"Do you see just how big The Big Blue Marble looks tonight, Talah? That's because, on rare occasions, it gets reeeally close to us, and that makes it look so much bigger. It almost feels as if it's trying to touch us - like it's trying to tell us something..."

Her story would continue, but at that moment Talah couldn't remember how, and that frustrated him beyond belief.

Talah didn't feel much like jumping these days. He couldn't help feeling a bit blue after discovering that there could be wolves like him down there.

"There **must** be a way to get to The Big Blue Marble..." he repeated to himself, "There has to be something we can do... something we're missing."

Talah knew how important this was for his mum. She'd spent years investigating; tracing plans, inventing all sorts of strange devices... all to find a way to The Big Blue Marble. And Hati, Talah's dad... he'd died trying to find a way there. It happened shortly after Talah was born: he'd left for one of his expeditions, but he never came back. Search parties looked for him for weeks, months... but he was nowhere to be found; and the Moon's wilderness is famous for its dangerous cliffs and bottomless pits.

Hati was considered one of the greatest explorers the Moon had ever known... but for Talah, he was much more than that – he was a hero... *his* hero.

But Talah had to focus now; he needed to bring his mind back to The Big Blue Marble... and then of course Mr Thomson appeared out of nowhere, with his grey, pinstriped hat on his head, as always.

"Daydreaming again, huh?" Mr Thomson grumbled as he walked past. No reply was given, but that didn't stop him. "You're being ridiculous. Time you grew up and stopped fantasising all day about jumping down to The Big Blue Marble! You've still got time to find your path and make something of your life; don't be like your mum and dad and waste it on those crazy dreams!"

Talah really, **reeeeally** tried not to let old Mr Thomson get to him, but the thought of Astorai wolves like him ridiculing his mum and dads' work made his blood **BOIL**... And In the end, he couldn't stop himself.

Talah's face frowned, and his teeth started to show. He was about to open his mouth to let out the fiercest growl when...

"BRRRRRRRRRRR..." that sound again... That **loud**, *rumbling* noise; like the sound of a freight train... Talah knew this all too well; he looked up to the sky and there it was; that bright light with a blazing trail of dust in its wake... another shooting star!

So many thoughts ran through Talah's mind. He wanted to prove to everyone that his mum and dad were right; he wanted to make them proud...

And then – he remembered. He remembered how his mum's words continued:

"Do you see just how big The Big Blue Marble looks tonight, Talah? That's because, on rare occasions, it gets reeeally close to us, and that makes it look so much bigger. It almost feels as if it's trying to touch us - like it's trying to tell us something..."

....

"... These are the Full Blue Marble nights, Son... if there's ever a time to jump so high that your snout'll touch the planet, that time is tonight!"

It was all so clear now; Talah knew exactly what he had to do. With lightning speed he stood up, legs and paws ready, chin up, and eyes fixed on the hurtling fireball. Talah had been preparing for this all his life. He was ready.

The shooting star drew nearer and nearer, Talah had to be as precise as clockwork if he wanted this to work. The star got closer, and **closer** and **closer** and...

"WOOOSH!" Talah jumped with the strength of a thousand wolves. In fact, he jumped so high that Mr Thomson jumped out of his skin, and his hat – which never left the top of his head– flew off and disappeared into space!

Talah felt like a shooting star himself, he soared **higher**, and **higher**... and landed on top of the star as it made its way to The Big Blue Marble!

The star felt warm and cosy; with colours so bright, a sound so deafening and a speed so insane that Talah had to grit his teeth and grip his claws right into its surface to hold on! He knew he should close his eyes, but he couldn't. He had the adventurous spirit of Lua and Hati, his mum and dad. He would take in **Every. Single. Second**.

The shooting star followed a clear path, and the many features of the planet could now be seen. The relentless ocean waves, the birds flying and singing in the sky, the trees dancing in the breeze... Talah had almost made it.

Next stop... **The Big Blue Marble!**

A New World

The shooting star was flying incredibly fast, and it had now a clear target.

The star was heading towards a massive rock in the middle of a forest, the same rock Talah saw through the telescope the night Lua told him about the Big Blue Marble wolves. It had a smooth, flat top; so wide and clear that it almost seemed as though it'd been designed for the star to land on it.

Talah felt the cold night air whisk through his fur as he drew rapidly closer to the rock, it would be a matter of seconds until he landed. He was a brave Astorai, but this thing had no brakes!

5... "Here we go."

4... Paws gripped tightly to the star.

3..."I'm not closing my eyes - I'm not missing the landing!" Talah said, gritting his teeth.

2...

1..."Ok maybe I'd better close my eyes." the young Astorai said, as he squeezed his eyes shut and braced for impact.

WOOOOOSSSSHHHHH!

All his life, Talah had dreamed about touching The Big Blue Marble with his snout... and now, he had!

In fact, the first part of his body to touch the ground was his snout... and it served quite well as a brake too!

It wasn't a perfect landing, but not bad for his first time. After making sure all his body parts were where they were meant to be, Talah started to dust himself off, but he quickly forgot about that when he looked up.

"Is that... home?" Talah asked himself as he saw the Moon. He knew the answer perfectly well, but he still couldn't believe what he'd just done.

It was so strange, Talah saw the same dark blue sky, and the same glowing stars as he could see from home, but now he couldn't see the Big Blue Marble... but the Moon!

"Hang on... **I'm on The Big Blue Marble!!!**" shouted Talah, as if he'd just realised where he was. Then he excitedly started looking and sniffing all around him.

It was a windy night, but his thick fur coat protected him from the cold. The trees... his mum had told him so much about the trees. They were alive, even if they didn't walk or talk, and there were so, **sooo** many of them! There was something incredibly beautiful about all of this, but Talah couldn't quite explain what it was.

It was only after marvelling at the beauty of the forest that Talah realised that the shooting star was there too. It was embedded deep into the rock, just where it'd just landed, but its glow had disappeared.

Talah tried to prize it out using his paws, fangs and tail, but no matter how hard he tried, the star just wouldn't move. After a gargantuan effort (and no small amount of panting), Talah stopped trying. He had more important things to do, anyway.

"Where exactly am I?" thought Talah while surveying the forest from the top of the rock. "And more importantly... Where are they?" he wondered, thinking of the wolves.

Talah took a deep breath of the fresh cold air and looked up at the Moon, up at his home.

"I will find them, Mum. For you and for Dad." Talah said softly.

And then, with a determined look on his face, the young Astorai started climbing down the rock. A thick, dark, slightly scary forest awaited him, and he would <u>not</u> back down.

Into the Wild

This forest was absolutely breathtaking. Used to the big never-ending plains and craters of the Moon, Talah marvelled at everything great and small that kept appearing and disappearing as he traversed the woods.

"There's a lot of green and brown on The Big Blue Marble!" thought Talah, as he counted tree number 236.

As he explored the labyrinth of wood and leaves, one thing impressed Talah more than anything else: the grass. It was like nothing he'd ever felt before. It felt soft and squishy, and its tiny blades tickled his toes. It smelled of life and water, and its dewdrops made Talah feel as if he were walking on a big green fuzzy wet rug.

A familiar noise caught Talah's attention; it sounded like a stream of water running somewhere nearby.

"I should've had something to eat before jumping on that star..." thought Talah as he raced towards the stream. His tummy was rumbling and his mouth was dry, he was both hungry *and* thirsty.

The stream turned out to be a wide river, and after running there, Talah realised that he was so much more tired than he would've been on the Moon. Things were certainly beautiful on The Big Blue Marble, but he had lost the lightness he felt back home.

The water from the river was crystal clear – even in the dead of night – and Talah lapped it up as if he wanted to drink the river dry. It was incredibly fresh.

"I should take some of this with me when I go home," thought Talah. But as he drank, another thought crossed his mind, and this one made him lift his head from the water and adopt a worried face. "Uh oh... How am I going to get back home???"

But Talah didn't have a chance to dwell on that. Out of the corner of his eye, he could see a shadow move through the trees, making a noise that he knew well. Paws padding through grass, leaves and branches... paws like his! But this shadow was on the other side of the river, and it was moving fast.

"I have to get across!" Talah decided quickly; and without losing track of the shadow, he started racing along his side of the riverbank.

The mysterious shadow was faster than him, and the distance between them grew greater by the minute. At this pace Talah would miss his chase. He had to do something, and do it **NOW**.

"Wait!" Talah screamed as he ran. "I just want to talk!" But the shadow didn't slow down.

Talah stared at the river, and the distance between the two banks.

"Guess I've no other option," thought Talah. "If I can jump on a shooting star... I can jump to the other side of this river!"

WOOSH!! Talah jumped as high and as far as he could...

.... But not far enough. **SPLASH!!**

Talah landed right into the deepest part of the river, where a strong current started dragging him along. He couldn't do much except fight to keep his head above water to breathe.

"How??!!… Why??!!… Why can't I just jump as far as on the Moon?? I feel so heavy!" Talah thought… and then he remembered another one of Lua's stories.

Talah remembered one night at the lighthouse, years ago. He was jumping about everywhere, just for the fun of it, but he also wouldn't stop looking at The Big Blue Marble through the window. Lua, seeing this, told him:

"You're lucky you live on the Moon, Talah… Down there on The Big Blue Marble, gravity is so strong that everyone and everything feels so much heavier! All the jumping and running you do here with such ease… you'd definitely have a much harder time doing that down there!"

But it was too late to learn from that lesson now. Talah had to focus on staying afloat… and **alive**.

The river seemed to end a bit further ahead. Talah could hear the roaring sound of crashing water, but couldn't see where. Little did he know, he was heading directly towards a waterfall.

His energy was draining fast. Talah was fighting with all his might, but the river was stronger. His eyes were closing, his mind was drifting... The water didn't feel so cold anymore.

Was he awake or was he dreaming? The last thing Talah could remember was the sight of a big, black figure waiting for him at the start of the waterfall...

It was a familiar figure – it was the figure of a **wolf**.

Far, Far Away

The whole Astorai community was in disbelief.

Either Mr Thomson had finally lost his mind, or all the wolves had been laughing at Lua when the joke was actually on them.

"I swear, Lua, I just saw your son jump onto a shooting star!" said Mr Thomson, sweating. His face formed a really silly expression out of fear, too.

Although extremely worried about the disappearance of her son, Lua showed more constraint and control over the situation than the grumpy, old wolf.

"When and where, Mr Thomson?" asked Lua.

"Just... just a few minutes ago, in the crater next to your lighthouse..." answered Mr Thomson. "I... I'm sorry Lua; we should've never doubted you... But what was Talah thinking!? What is he trying to prove!? He's putting himself in danger! And now he's disappeared!"

"Thank you, Mr Thomson." finished Lua, as she calmly left the lighthouse. The old wolf was surprised at the cool head Lua was displaying, but as soon as she was out of his sight, she started running towards the crater as fast as she could.

"Where are you, Son?" thought Lua, as she looked and sniffed for even the tiniest clue in the crater she knew Talah loved to play in – anything that may lead her to her son's whereabouts... And then a crazy idea stormed into her head.

"Can it be true? Did you actually get onto your shooting star, Talah?" Lua didn't notice, but half a smile formed on her face.

"But where did you go?" Lua asked herself, both worried and proud.

Her eyes immediately darted to The Big Blue Marble, and the half smile turned into a full one.

Talah's family, after all, were a family of **_adventurers!_**

Familiar Faces

It was a lovely morning. Talah woke up in a bed in a small, round cave. It was warm. The sunlight illuminated the beautiful rock walls and a chorus of birds was chirping harmoniously outside.

"Where... where am I?" thought Talah.

Well, for starters, he was alive, which is more than he expected when he lost consciousness in the river.

Talah quickly looked around – someone else lived there. There were beds - three of them - but no one to be seen or heard.

"I have to get up. I need to find the wolves and get back home... but how am I gonna do that!?" is all Talah could think of... until a loud, high-pitched bark disrupted his thoughts.

"WOOF, WOOF, WOOF!"

The sound came from inside the cave, but no one was there... Not until Talah decided to look down.

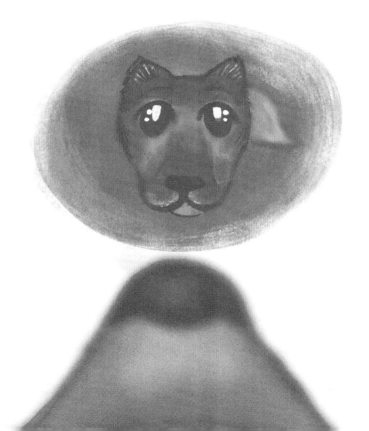

A tiny wolf cub was barking at him, eyes as big as plates that couldn't hide their excitement.

Although small, this cub was devilishly **FAST**! He ran about haphazardly, but after a few playful rolls he started barking at two figures that appeared at the entrance of the cave....

"WOOF, WOOF, WOOF!!!"

Talah found himself lying in front of two Big Blue Marble wolves (two and a half, if you count the little sprinter). He couldn't believe his eyes! Talah had planned this for so long, he wanted to meet the Big Blue Marble wolves more than anything... but now he was frozen still.

The couple slowly started walking towards Talah, and they looked so much like Moon wolves. They were around the same size as Talah's mum, and this made him think of how this whole adventure would be affecting her.

Talah tried to sit up, but he felt too weak. That rough landing on The Big Blue Marble, the cold windy night, running and swimming in this new heavy gravity... All of that drained his energy.

After watching Talah's failed attempts to sit up, one of the wolves dished out a bowl of food from a small fire in the corner of the cave and brought it to Talah. This was clearly a she-wolf, and her fur was the colour of copper and snow.

The aroma from the bowl smelled familiar.

"Chicken soup! You have chicken soup here on The Big Blue Marble! It's my favourite!" exclaimed Talah, looking at the couple, but they didn't answer. They seemed to be.... confused.

"My name is Talah," he continued, while lapping up the food like there was no tomorrow. "Thank you for bringing me here... and for the soup; it's so good!"

The couple looked at each other for a few seconds, and then back at Talah. The other wolf had grey fur with a bluish tinge, and he started talking:

"Woof woof...woof? Woof woof, woof woof woof woof. Woof woof woof?''

Talah's face froze, his mouth open. He could've kept speaking, but he realised it wouldn't do much good.

It was obvious. Even on the Moon, Astorai wolves from different parts spoke different languages. Talah was now on another planet, so these Big Blue Marble wolves had their own language.

Putting the bowl to one side, Talah pointed at himself with one of his paws, and said:

"Talah... My name is, Talah"

The couple looked at each other again. After a brief silence, they looked back at Talah.

"Selina," said the copper and snow wolf.

"Viggo," said the blue-grey wolf.

Talah couldn't believe it. He was talking to Big Blue Marble wolves!

"Danny!" screamed the bolting cub, still sprinting in circles around the cave.

But there was someone missing. The black wolf he saw last night right before he blacked out... he wasn't here. Talah didn't know how to ask the family about him, or how he was going to explain anything to them... let alone that he was from the Moon!

But Talah had a mission. He'd made it to this planet, and met the Big Blue Marble wolves. Now, he had to go back home and prove to everyone that his mum and dad were right all along!

The Smell of the Forest

Talah and the family of wolves were getting along fantastically well. In just a couple of days since he woke up in that cave, Talah had regained his strength and full health thanks to Selina and Viggo's great care.

He and the family went for strolls through the forest daily, and they taught him all there was to know about it. They showed him how to catch fish, how to swim in the pools, how to navigate his way through the woods... everything. There was a language barrier, for sure, but that didn't stop them learning from each other and having loads of fun doing it.

Talah felt the Moon and The Big Blue Marble couldn't be more different. Back home, everything was much more silent and calm, while down here everything seemed to happen at a much faster pace. But Talah found out something quite unexpected; wolves were all the same, regardless of where they came from. At the end of the day, all they wanted to do was to run, jump and enjoy the world they live in!

On his third night on The Big Blue Marble, Talah was taking the family to the big rock in the centre of the forest. He wanted to show them the embedded shooting star.

"Catch me!" screamed Talah, as he sprinted, dodging through trees.

"AAAAAAAAAAAGHHHH!!!" gurgled Danny. He hadn't quite mastered the language yet, (either the Big Blue Marble or the Moon one), but Talah could tell he was having fun.

Talah, Selina and Viggo ran like the wind through the woods, but somehow that little cub five or six times smaller than them was even faster. How Danny could run like that was a mystery to the whole wolf community.

Before they knew it, they'd all arrived at the big rock; and its highest point looked as if it were touching the Moon.

"This is where I landed! From the Moon!" said Talah.

Selina and Viggo gazed at the big rock, mesmerized as if it were the first time they'd seen it. Danny just tilted his head.

"Want to see a shooting star?" asked Talah, looking at Danny. Talah knew he wouldn't understand, so he lifted his paw and pointed to the top of the rock. Danny shot towards it like a cannon ball. He was pretty much a lighting bolt on command.

It took Talah, Selina and Viggo about ten minutes to get to the top of the rock. By the time they got there, Danny had sniffed every piece of rock, but there was no shooting star to be seen.

"How??"... It was here, it was right here! Embedded in the rock!" exclaimed Talah.

The star had disappeared, and there wasn't even a dent in the ground.

"I swear I landed here! I came from the Moon!" said Talah, racing around, looking for any trace of the star. "You have to believe me! I need to get back home! I, I have tell my mum all about you! I've been here for days, she must be really worried!"

The wolf family couldn't understand Talah's words, but they could see how upset he was. Selina looked at the Moon and then walked towards Talah to hug him. Viggo and Danny followed soon after.

Although this wasn't Talah's real family, and he missed Lua more than anything, these Blue

Marble wolves had been so good to him. For a brief moment, he felt calm.

"Woof, Talah...woof woof woof woof woof woof, woof woof woof woof woof woof woof." said Viggo.

Talah couldn't understand much, but he knew that roughly translated to:

"Come on, Talah... you've had a long day, let's get you some warm chicken soup."

(At least... he *HOPED* it involved chicken soup!)

It was late, the Sun would be rising in just a few hours, and Talah knew he wouldn't get back home tonight. Following Selina, Viggo and Danny, Talah walked down the rock and back to the cave, but this hadn't weakened his determination. He **would** find a way back home... with or without a shooting star.

The Long Watch

The days went by...

Talah thoroughly enjoyed his time with the Blue Marble wolves discovering the many wonders of this planet, but he also longed for his home on the Moon.

Every night, when the stars started to light the dark blue sky, Talah sneaked out of the cave and went back to the big rock. He climbed all the way to the peak, and there he stared at the Moon and the sky, searching for a way to get back home...

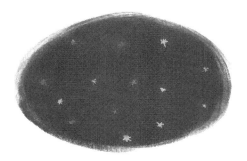

But Talah was never alone. Danny barely slept, and always caught him sneaking out of the cave. Talah usually wouldn't even know that Danny was following him, but by the time he reached the peak of the rock, Danny would already be there, looking at the Moon. Turns out, that besides being insanely fast, Danny could also be quite silent when he wanted to be!

Tonight, like every other night for weeks now, Talah was looking at the Moon, with Danny next to him.

"It's funny... When I was on the Moon, I had a favourite spot in a crater where I could sit for hours; gazing at The Big Blue Marble, thinking of ways to get here." said Talah.

Danny seemed to be mesmerised by the sky, but Talah knew he was listening too.

"And now here I am, on my favourite spot on The Big Blue Marble, gazing at the Moon and thinking of ways to get back there..."

For one minute, Danny and Talah sat there on top of the big rock, in silence. It felt as if The Big Blue Marble had commanded her rivers and winds to be silent to give Talah some peace – the kind of peace he so fondly remembered from home. So right there and then, just for a minute, Talah almost felt as if he were back home...

But this calm wouldn't last long.

A raindrop fell on Talah's snout, and many more followed.

   "I didn't know it rained here on The Big Blue Marble too, Danny." said Talah.

Talah suddenly saw fear in Danny's eyes and ears. He saw him putting his tail between his legs and starting to retreat down the rock.

   "Don't be afraid, Danny, it's just a bit of ra-"

CCCRRRRRRRRRRRRRRRRRR...

A **BOLT OF LIGHTNING** as thick as an oak tree tore the sky apart, followed by tremendous thunder that shook the big rock itself. All of a sudden, Talah realised that Danny's decision to run back home was the right one.

He wanted to stay on the rock for longer, looking for signs, but he couldn't leave Danny alone, not in this storm.

As Talah ran down the rock to catch Danny, he felt a presence behind him... He looked back, but could see nothing. The rain, the leaves battered by the wind, the darkness of the night... Talah couldn't see further than the end of his own snout... but then another lighting bolt struck. Now he could see it: the silhouette of a wolf at the top of the rock, the same wolf he'd seen as he fought for his life in the river... **The Black Wolf**.

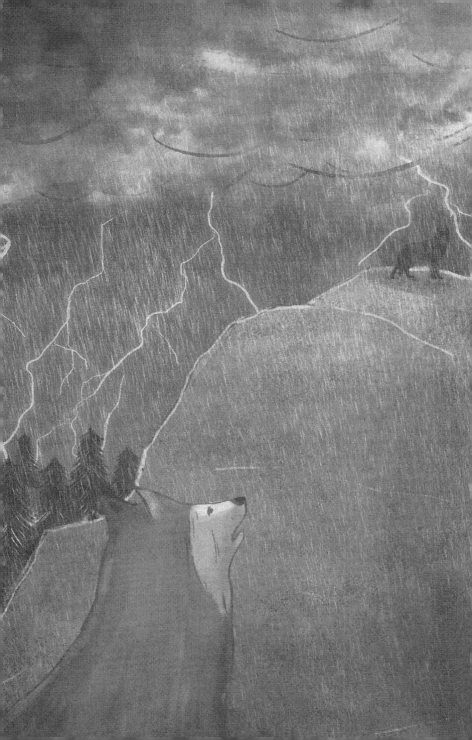

Talah tried to turn back to the wolf; he felt this urge to get closer to him, but then...

"AaAaAAaaaAAAaaaaAAaARGHHHH!!!" Danny screamed.

Talah instinctively ran towards the cub, jumping from one part of the rock to another.

Danny was trapped under some thick branches. The wind was so wild, so strong, that it was uprooting even the tallest trees. But Danny had been lucky; he had just got buried under some leaves and wasn't actually hurt, probably thanks to his small size.

"I'm gonna get you out, Danny, c'mon!" cried Talah as he moved all the branches away.

Danny looked stunned, but not afraid.

Grabbing Danny by the scruff of the neck, Talah tossed him over his head and onto his back.

"We're riding back to the cave, Danny." Talah said, trying to calm Danny down. And it seemed to work. The tiny cub looked more aware of the fun of riding on Talah's back than the danger they were in.

And so, Talah and Danny rode back to the little cave in the woods, hoping to sneak back into their beds... But they were out of luck.

Talah thought nothing could be more terrifying than that storm, but as he crept into the cave, his eyes met Selina and Viggo's and he realised he was wrong. He was in trouble. **BIG TIME!**

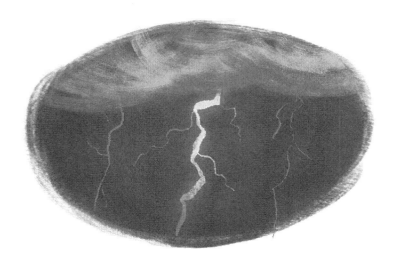

Heavy Machinery

Lua hadn't stopped looking for ways to contact Talah since the day Mr Thomson came rushing in to tell her about Talah's disappearance. As a matter of fact, the whole wolf community rallied round to help with the search.

"Bring me the sicolapterus!"

"Check the primaris levels!"

"DO NOT touch that button!"...

These were just a few of the many, many orders that Lua barked at the wolves assisting with a secret construction of hers inside the lighthouse.

Mr Thomson, like every other wolf involved in the project, had no idea what any of these words meant or what it was they were helping to build, but they still helped her as best they could.

"Lua... do you have a moment?" Mr Thomson asked, as she was tightening screws on some heavy machinery she was working on.

"Of course, Mr Thomson, what is it?" she replied, without taking her eyes off her work.

"I... I think I never properly apologised, Lua." continued Mr Thomson.

Lua kept working, but now seemed more interested in the conversation.

"I... I'm sorry. I never gave you and your husband a chance to prove yourselves... To be honest, we're all sorry. We all treated you like a couple of nutcases, but we were the ones who were wrong all along." Mr Thomson finished, hanging his head low.

"I appreciate your apology, Mr Thomson, and I accept it. But… you all rallied round to come help me build this: I count that as apology enough." replied Lua.

Mr Thomson's eyes brightened, as if a big weight had been lifted from his shoulders.

"Thank you, Lua… But that brings me to another question… I… We… We were wondering, what is it exactly that we're building here?" Mr Thomson asked; looking at the massive piece of metal and glass Lua was working on.

Putting her tools aside, Lua moved closer to Mr Thomson. Like him, she looked at the massive piece of metal and glass; but in her face there was pride, not curiosity.

"This, Mr Thomson, is what's going to bring Talah back home."

Into the Breach

Talah didn't need to be fluent in Blue Marble language to understand what Selina and Viggo were saying this time.

"You can't just disappear like that!"

"The forest isn't safe at night!"

"These storms are dangerous!"

"You could have died!!"...

He and Danny were grounded. They spent the day after their previous nights escape polishing every small stone and stick in the cave, and were forbidden from leaving it.

"AaAaAaAaaaaAAaaA!!" Danny cried over and over again.

"I know, Danny, I know... But we have to make sure we don't get on your mum and dad's bad side again..." replied Talah.

More than anything, Talah wanted to get out of the cave and continue his search for a way back home, but he felt he deserved the punishment. He couldn't have known about these violent storms on The Big Blue Marble, but he'd put Danny in danger. There would be no venturing out of the cave today...

And so the morning passed. The afternoon did too. And the evening was well on its way. Through it all, the positively terrifying storm still raged on; and the lightning that struck near the cave made Danny jump in fear and race to hide under his bed.

"Don't worry, Danny, you're safe now." said Viggo, as he stroked the cub's head to calm him down.

But Talah felt unsettled. He couldn't stop watching the storm from within the cave. It was late, and completely dark outside, but the thunderstorm brought in flashes of blinding light. He knew venturing out would be dangerous, but he felt as if he *had* to…

"This is a very dangerous night, Talah," said Selina, who had been looking at him attentively. She sensed somehow that he wanted to get out there again. "I can assure you, being out there right now in this storm… it'd be the end of you."

After all these weeks, Talah could barely speak the Blue Marble Wolves' language, but he could understand it well.

"This is no ordinary storm, Talah. Tonight, every wolf in the forest; big or small, weak or strong, will be staying inside their caves. The rain cascades down like a waterfall, the wind thrashes against the trees and the thunder is deafening... These are the Full Moon storms, and we're lucky that they're rare." continued Selina, deep in thought.

Talah felt a sudden rush of adrenaline.

"A Full Moon??" exclaimed Talah. "Of course!!!"

It all made sense now. Talah knew what he had to do and wanted to tell the family all about his plan.

"Me... woof woof have to go woof woof home woof, woof woof Full Moon woof woof **NOW!**" said Talah, knowing he couldn't make them understand the whole story.

"I'll miss you..." Talah finished in his own language, hoping they might understand.

Viggo and Selina looked at Talah, worried and confused, and they weren't fast enough to catch him when he sprinted out of the cave.

"TALAH!!!" Selina shouted.

But it was too late. Without looking back, Talah had disappeared into the storm... and something told her that he wouldn't be back.

One Last Climb

Talah was running faster than ever before. His muscles were tense and his breath short; he knew he didn't have much time.

"The Full Moon... of course it was the Full Moon!" thought Talah, as he dodged trees and fallen branches.

"I came to The Big Blue Marble on the night it was closest to the Moon, on the night of the Full Blue Marble... I needed the Moon to be the closest to The Big Blue Marble to get back!"

But Talah couldn't afford to dwell on his theory; he had to focus on getting back to the big rock.

Selina and Viggo didn't exaggerate about the storm; every step Talah took was a dangerous one. The rain was still torrential, and the ground muddy. If he weren't careful, he'd get trapped in one of the many dirt puddles.

"A shooting star will appear tonight. I'll be home before the night ends!" Talah repeated to himself, as he dodged fallen trees and puddles with ease thanks to his talent for jumping.

But for that to happen, he had to reach the rock on time. It was already quite late when he left the cave, the night would end soon… And with it, the Full Moon.

The thick foliage of the trees and the heavy clouds in the sky shielded Talah from almost any light. He was galloping as fast as he could, his face constantly being hit by a seemingly endless maze of leaves, branches and twigs - making even the air hard to breathe. Talah was disoriented. The forest was a dark, dangerous place tonight.

For what felt like an eternity, the young Astorai raced through the woods. He found himself running in circles on many occasions, and the fear of missing his one chance to reach the top of the big rock before the night ended made his heart pound.

"Am I even running in the right direction?" Talah said thoughtfully. "I can barely se-..." The smell of fresh air behind some trees in front of him muted his words. He started sniffing his way towards them.

Talah exhaled in relief. Finally, it was the end of the forest. Now a clearing and a huge rock stood in front of him – bigger and **darker** than he'd remembered.

Rain and clouds blackened the sky. Talah couldn't see the Moon, although he knew it was there, he could feel it. So Talah planted one paw on the big rock, then a second, a third and a forth... and started his climb...

The wind felt like a stampede, pulling Talah back and screaming at him, warning him to give up. His whole body was drenched in rainwater, making the climb feel as if he were carrying the world on his shoulders. It was tough... but so was he. Talah could see the peak of the rock.

"Mum will be mad at me, and with good reason... But I have to show her that we can travel to The Big Blue Marble, **and back!**" thought Talah, determined. These positive thoughts kept him going. He knew that the moment he gave himself a second to rest, or to dwell on his fears, he would collapse.

Talah's sore paws reached the top of the big rock. Somehow, he was expecting it to be better up there; but the rain, the wind and the lightning reigned there too.

Unexpectedly, something put a smile on Talah's face. It was there. The silhouette of the Moon!

And it was fighting to break through the dark clouds to shine down on him.

"Any time now. All I have to do is look at the sky and focus on getting back home, the shooting star will come!" Talah said to himself. And for what felt like an eternity, Talah waited and waited at the top of the rock, exposed to the fury of the Full Moon storm.

Talah kept thinking of the star, the Moon, his home and his mum, in that order. He longed to be back home more than anything, but... no shooting star was coming to his rescue.

"C'mon... I know you're out there... show yourself!" gnarled Talah through gritted teeth.

The cold winds on his wet fur were starting to take too much of a toll on him. He didn't know how much longer he could hold on like this.

"It can't end like this... I have to prove my parents life work... I have to get back to my mum... COME ON!!" he shouted... But nothing happened...

...

......

Until... **it did**.

The Moon suddenly broke through the clouds, shining brighter than ever.

"Mum!" Talah exclaimed, not realising that the word had slipped out of his mouth.

Talah's eyes frantically darted all over the sky for the star – now much clearer since the clouds were being pushed away – but he found himself searching for his home: for his lighthouse on the Moon.

"Focus on the star, Talah! Home is still so far away, you're not gonna see it from here, not without a telescope like the one mum has!" he thought.

Talah tried everything in his power: he scanned the skies incessantly, he sniffed the air for even the tiniest hint, he even tried to scratch the rock in search of the missing shooting star, but... no sign of it. The storm was hitting as hard as a sledgehammer. Talah could barely feel his own paws anymore... and time was running out.

"I'm sorry, Mum..." said Talah, looking at the Moon, talking to Lua – wherever she was.

Dropping onto his paws, Talah closed his eyes. This storm was grinding down his spirit. It was getting too much.

"I should never have left my crater... I should never have left our home... I should never have left your side..." he continued... but a spark kindled in Talah's heart.

A burst of memories of him with his mum came rushing to his mind. Talah thought himself a fearless explorer, but he missed Lua more than anything.

He remembered a time when he was just a cub like Danny. He was in the lighthouse, in front of the main door trying to stop Lua from leaving the house. She had to go on an expedition for a month to find materials to build the telescope she had now.

"Be brave, Talah. Now you're the wolf of the house, I know you'll guard it valiantly while I'm away." said Lua, with the warmest smile on her face.

But Talah didn't seem too convinced.

"Son, you know I have to go... This expedition will take me far away from home, but you also know I'll come back. And when I do, there'll be nothing I'll want more than to hug you and tell you all about it!" continued Lua.

Talah took a second to compose himself. He was sad about his mum going away, but also proud of her.

"I'll... I'll miss you, Mum..." replied Talah, holding back a tear.

Lua looked Talah in the eye, with that lovely warm smile she always had for him.

"Come, Son, there's something I want to show you." said Lua.

And so, they walked towards the attic, to the big terrace from which they could see the vast plains, hills and craters of the Moon. No matter how many times they saw them, they always marvelled at the beauty of their homeland. Lua got closer to Talah to press her head against his, and said:

"Whenever you feel alone, whenever you miss me… howl for me. Wherever you are, I promise… I'll always hear you."

Talah shook his head.

The rain was blinding him, so he squinted. The wind was pushing him back, so he stood back up and gripped the ground firmly with his paws. The thunder was roaring at him to leave this place… *so he replied:*

On Top of the World

It was a busy night at the lighthouse.

"How are we doing with the magnifying glasses?" Lua shouted at the wolves working on her machine.

"Almost ready!" muffled voices replied from beneath the massive structure.

"We don't have much more time, we have to finish it tonight! I need the promethium liquid to be rea-" Lua stopped her sentence abruptly; she could've sworn she heard something coming from outside the lighthouse, from outside the plains, hills and craters. From... *outer space*.

Walking purposefully towards her son's favourite crater, Lua fixed her eyes on The Big

Blue Marble. There was a special glow in those eyes, and with hope in her heart, she looked at the blue planet and gasped:

"Is that you, Son?"

"**Awooo... awooooooo... awoooooooooo!!**" Talah howled.

"'I love you, and I miss you', is what it means when we howl." Lua told Talah that night a long time ago when he was just a cub.

And love her and miss her, he did.

But the storm was howling too – so fiercely that it drowned out any sound coming from Talah.

"Mum won't hear me above this storm, I have to do something," Talah thought, determined to reach Lua's ears.

So he walked towards the end of the big rock, to the point where his paws were right on the edge. One wrong move and the fall would be catastrophic, but Talah was willing to take the risk.

"Awooooooooooooooooo!!!" Talah shouted at the skies, defying all the forces of nature.

"Awoooooooooooooooooooooooooooooo!!!!!!!!" he continued, his howl threatening to silence the thunder...

.... But thunder replied.

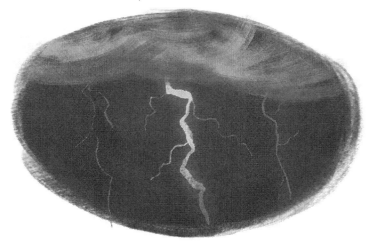

A bolt of lightning hit the cliff's edge; making the piece of rock Talah was standing on collapse and crumble. The impact momentarily dazzled him, and by the time his vision came back, it was too late. The rock was fragmenting and falling into the abyss – and Talah was going down with it.

"NO! It *CAN'T* end like this." Talah thought as he was falling down the cliff... but he was a quick thinker.

Talah's eyes spied a branch sticking out of the big rock, and he quickly turned and grabbed it with his teeth.

"URGHH... I have to get back up there." Talah said to himself between gritted teeth, holding the branch preventing him from falling into the darkness.

He tried to grip the rock with his paws. He swung his body from one side to the other to reach a sure footing, but nothing got him closer to safety... and his jaws were getting tired.

Suddenly, a sound came from above...

"Awoooooo..." resounded through the air. *"Awoooooooooo..."* voices from the top of the rock howled

His jaws couldn't hold on anymore, he was slipping off the branch... but just as his grip slipped off, just as he was falling into the abyss... a set of wolf teeth grabbed him by the neck and lifted him back onto the big rock.

His whole body gratefully embraced the ground and he exhaled in relief, but his breath left him again when he lifted his gaze up from the ground.

The Black Wolf stood in front of him. He was much bigger up close, and even though he had just saved Talah from certain death, he was the one who looked grateful.

"Thank you..." Talah said, still in disbelief. "I wish you could understand me. I owe you my life!"

"...And I owe you mine, Son." the black wolf replied... in Astorai language!

Talah eyes grew as wide as the Moon itself.

"Son?? Are you... are you??..." Talah stammered. He did so not only because of the black wolf's words, but because now, from up close, Talah could spot small flecks of silver running through his fur. The undeniable mark of an *Astorai*.

The black wolf pressed his head against Talah's, just as Lua would do.

"All will become clear soon, Son, I promise... but we don't have much time now. There's something you have to do," the black wolf said as he eyed the top of the rock. "... And this time, you won't be alone."

Talah instinctively turned around; he felt dozens of eyes on him.

They were all there: Selina, Viggo, Danny and it looked like every other wolf in the forest. Why or how, Talah didn't know; but now he felt ten times stronger. And so, with his new-found strength, the young Moon wolf took a deep breath and...

"**Awooooooooooooooooooooooo!!!!!!!**" he howled.

All of a sudden, a ray of light peaked out from the clouds and started moving all across the forest. This was no ordinary light, and it looked as if it were looking for something... or some**_one_**.

Talah knew that kind of light. It was light only a lighthouse could cast... and it wasn't coming from the clouds... it was coming from the Moon!

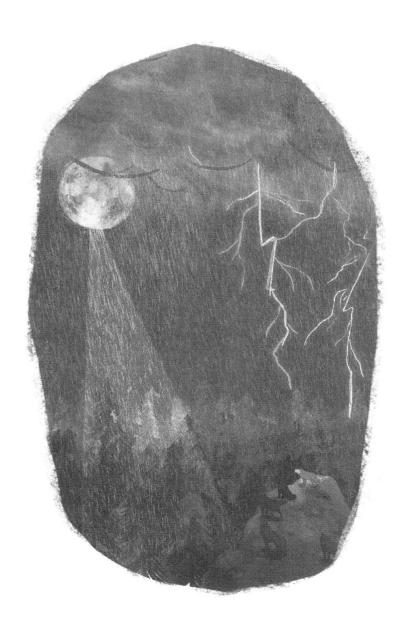

The First Howl

Back on the Moon, the search was frantic.

The secret new machine was finished. It was a HUMONGOUS searchlight that sat above the observatory, and its beam was so bright and powerful that it could pinpoint a place on The Big Blue Marble like a ray of light coming straight from the Sun.

"Where to, Captain?" Mr Thomson inquired, "The storm is too wild and widespread, I can't see a thing!" he continued, as he cranked gears and cogs in the machine, casting the light down towards the storm area on The Big Blue Marble.

"15 degrees north, Mr Thomson. The howling came from the forest, he can't be far!" Lua replied.

A pack of thirty wolves (plus Mr Thomson) were operating all sorts of strange knobs and buttons on the new machine. All of them working with one purpose and one purpose only: to find Talah.

"Damn that storm... I know you're somewhere down there..." Lua said to herself, as she surveyed The Big Blue Marble from her command board.

"*Whenever you feel alone, whenever you miss me... howl for me. Wherever you are, I promise... I'll always hear you.*" Lua had told Talah all those years ago, and she wasn't going to break that promise.

Howling at the Moon

The light cast from the Moon was moving incessantly all over the forest. Talah *knew* it was Lua searching for him, but he also knew that with this storm she would never find him. He needed to give her something else, something to pinpoint his location... and he knew exactly what to do.

With steely determination, Talah walked up to the edge of the cliff, and stood with the Moon covering him as a mantle.

"I don't know if I'll make it back home, Mum..." Talah said, looking at the light. "But I want you to know that you were right... There *ARE* wolves on The Big Blue Marble, wolves just like us... And I would never have seen them if it weren't for you. I love you, and I miss you, Mum."

The rain didn't bother Talah anymore. The wind wasn't strong enough for Talah anymore... He stretched his head back to look the Moon right in the eye, and...

"*AWOOOOOOOOOOOOOOOO!!!!!!!*"

The thunder cowered under the might of his howl.

The rest of the pack joined him in an amazing chorus of howls, silencing the war cry of the storm. None of them knew why they were howling, none of them had even howled before... but they all instinctively felt they *had* to. After hearing Talah's first howl all over the forest, they felt compelled to run towards it. They all felt something inside them that made them want to face the dark blue sky, take a deep breath, and howl at the Moon... And surprisingly, it was Danny who had the most powerful pipes! And no-one dared break his concentration.

The storm was settling down. A sense of tranquillity fell over the big rock, and Talah felt as if the howling had brought that about. It was fighting the clouds, the rain and the wind, bringing them closer to what they all felt drawn to: The Moon. And hearing the wolves' song... the Moon *answered*.

The light that was frantically moving all over the forest now fell upon the big rock; illuminating it and bringing warmth to the wolves that were there. But for Talah, there was something else in store.

"Son!" the black wolf exclaimed in disbelief, and Talah turned around to look at him.

The shooting star was there again. The shooting star that brought him to the Big Blue Marble so long ago was there, embedded into the ground, as if it had never left.

"I thought I'd never see it again..." the black wolf said, his eyes welling up.

The star wasn't glowing in the slightest, it seemed as if it were dead, but Talah still saw the wolves' faces entranced by it. Some of them, the ones beside the black wolf, were looking at the shooting star as if they were seeing an old friend.

"What... what's going on?" Talah asked Hati, pretty much in disbelief himself.v

"This is the shooting star that brought me here too, Son... just like it brought you." Hati replied, composing himself. "Your mother and I spent our lives working to prove the existence of wolves on The Big Blue Marble. When the shooting star appeared to me during that expedition all those years ago... I had to do it - I felt compelled to jump on it."

Talah was listening to him amazed and confused at the same time.

"C'mon! Give your old man some credit! Who do you think you got that talent from, eh??"

Hati teased Talah, as he lightly punched him on the shoulder.

"But... But why're all these wolves looking at the star as if they've seen it before?" Talah asked.

"When I got here, I discovered that we weren't the first ones to jump on shooting stars, Son.." Hati continued. "I've spent all these years looking for other Moon wolves, hoping one day I'd be able to bring them back home... but we never discovered how. We thought we'd see out the rest of our days on this planet."

Talah took a few seconds to think, and said:

"Then why... why didn't you come for me? I saw you across the river the night I first arrived on The Big Blue Marble, and then I saw you again the night the storm started... Why... why did you avoid me?"

Hati looked down for a second, thinking carefully of his next words, and said:

"Maybe because I was afraid... Never finding a way back home has been haunting me every year I've spent here, Son. For our people, I disappeared without a trace on that expedition. Your mother probably thinks I'm dead, and that's something I can never forgive myself for... and you were only a few weeks old when I disappeared - you'd barely even opened your eyes... but when I saw that star coming down from the sky, I don't know how, but I just *knew* it was you."

Talah was about to say something, but Hati continued:

"At first I couldn't bear the thought of you, my only son, getting stuck here as I did... but then I realised... You are the son of Lua and Hati, the crazy astronomers that live in a lighthouse. Exploring is in our blood! If anyone could take us back home, if anyone could find a way back to the Moon... it was going to be you, Son!!... But I too knew that you would have to discover how to do that by yourself... so I did the one thing that a father can do: I looked after you. I made sure you got out of that river alive, and made sure that you and Danny got back to the cave in one piece,"

Talah was lost for words.

"You've done what no other wolf has ever done, Son. You were smart enough to work out that we can only get back home on the day of the Full Moon, and you've been strong enough to defeat the storm that stopped us from seeing the path... You've saved us."

Lunging forward, Hati hugged Talah tightly, and uttered eight words that made Talah (for the first time in his life), realise that he had a father.

"I couldn't be more proud of you, Son."

Father and son embraced each other. And the shooting star, that seemed to be dead, started to glow and shudder, as if it were trying to release itself from the ground.

Feeling the warmth that it gave off, Talah smiled; and looking back at Hati, said:

"We're going back home, Dad."

Space Wolves

Hati and a pack of twelve Astorai wolves stood next to the glowing shooting star waiting for Talah, who had a bittersweet moment to go through.

"Have some of this before you leave, the way back to the Moon must be a long one." said Viggo, as he put down a bowl of chicken soup for Talah (that got emptied pretty quickly!)

"Aaaaah???...Aaahhhh..." said Danny, not especially hyperactively for the first time ever.

"I'll miss you all." Talah replied, holding back a tear. "If... If I could ever come back to visit-"

"Your Blue Marble family will be here, waiting for you." Selina added, finishing his sentence.

Talah threw himself in to hug them, and for the duration of it, even Danny stood silent.

"You have to go! The night is almost through!" Selina exclaimed, breaking the group hug and pretending she wasn't emotional.

Talah smiled at them wishing he could be in two places at once. With a heavy heart, he turned back to the shooting star, still embedded in the ground.

Of the twelve Astorai, only half of them stayed by the star. The other half, after looking at it one last time with a smile on their face and a tear in their eye, walked back down to join the Blue Marble wolves.

"Dad," Talah said, pointing at the Astorai wolves that left the star. "Aren't they coming with us?"

"No, Son. Some of them have been on The Big Blue Marble for far, far longer than I have, and have families here now." Hati replied, looking at them one last time. "In the end, it doesn't matter where you are, what matters is that you're with those that make you *feel* like you're home."

Talah took a moment to look at the vast forest around him. The wind was now a nice breeze caressing his fur, and he could hear the clear song of the rivers, trees and animals. He took a deep breath, and said:

"Time to go home."

And with that, the six old Moon wolves, Hati and Talah jumped on the star. With a display of wonder, it sparkled and grew in size, providing space for all of them to comfortably sit on it…. but it didn't move.

"Talah…?" Hati said looking at his son, who only had three of his four legs on the star.

Talah smiled, and after a moment of silence, popped his fourth leg onto the star. And there it was again; that loud, rumbling noise, like the sound of a freight train.

The star broke free from the rock and hovered over the ground, Talah could feel it getting ready to launch itself into space, so he said:

"Get a good grip of it! This is gonna-"

"Go really fast??? Yes, we know!" said the oldest wolf amongst them, who now had the most childishly-excited expression on his face.

Talah was about to laugh when the shooting star rocketed **up** and **away** at *INSANE* speed.

It left a trail of glowing golden light behind it, and the Blue Marble wolves watching would never forget that spectacle.

......

....

....

First, Talah could see the whole rock.

Then, he could see the forest, rivers and mountains...

Finally, Talah saw the whole Big Blue Marble below him.

It was hard to stop looking down, but he started looking up...

First, Talah could see the whole Moon before him.

Then, he saw the craters, plains and mountains...

Finally, Talah saw his little lighthouse.

I love you, and I miss you

"Are the ribbunum radars working? Any sign yet?" Lua shouted at the wolves working on the machines.

"Negative, Captain" a panting voice replied from below. "That thing heading towards us is casting too bright a light, we can't see anything!"

"Fix it! We need to know what happened back th-" Lua continued, until a noise coming from outside the lighthouse made her freeze. A loud, rumbling noise; like the sound of a freight train.

The wolves were starting to get used to seeing Lua leave the building mid-sentence, but this time it was different. This time they just heard a resounding *"Talah!"*, and by the time they looked at the command board where she usually was, there was no sign of her. She was out in her son's favourite crater.

Lua couldn't believe her eyes. A gigantic, powerful fireball coming from outer space came hurtling towards her at insane speed. Before she could react, it smashed into the ground, making a new crater and forming a massive glowing cloud of sparks, light and dust.

The sheer impact **THREW** Lua backwards, making her tumble and fall. A pack of wolves were forming behind her, and Mr Thomson rushed to help her back up. He had a new grey, pinstriped hat on his head, but after lifting Lua back up, he looked at the glowing cloud and slowly, with great care, he took it off.

Lua couldn't see anything, the cloud was too thick... but she knew what was inside it. So she called for it to come out.

"Awooooooooooo..." she howled, softly...

And a young wolf covered in dust emerged from the rubble, saying:

"I love you, and I've missed you too, Mum."

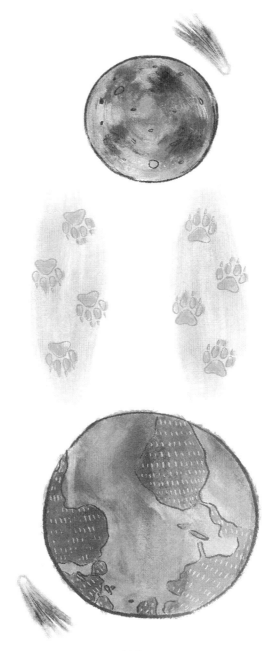

Epilogue

Millennia passed. The world changed, and continues to change in so many ways... but we humans still marvel at wolves howling.

So now, at night, whenever you're lucky enough to see a wolf walk to the highest peak; look up to the sky and howl at the Moon, know that you're witnessing the meeting of two old friends. For their connection runs deeper than we will ever understand.

Know that somewhere, a wolf still remembers. Know that, maybe, the shooting star you see blazing in the sky is Talah, coming back to visit his friends on this good Earth... or to take them back with him so they can explore, run and jump together.

Maybe you should howl too, for who knows... Maybe one day, you could explore, run and jump with him too.

Printed by Amazon Italia Logistica S.r.l.
Torrazza Piemonte (TO), Italy

24421916R00068